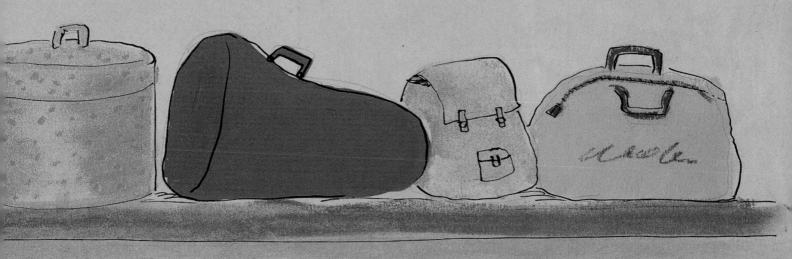

Text copyright © 2004 by Harriet Ziefert
Illustrations copyright © 2004 by Emily Bolam
All rights reserved / CIP Data is available.
Published in the United States 2004 by
🍎 Blue Apple Books
515 Valley Street, Maplewood, N.J. 07040
www.blueapplebooks.com
Distributed in the U.S. by Chronicle Books
Printed in China
First Edition
ISBN: 1-59354-066-3
1 3 5 7 9 10 8 6 4 2

Page 17
Photo credit: Eric Lessing/Art Resource, NY.
Photo credit: Réunion des Musées Nationaux / Art Resource, NY.
Photo credit: Réunion des Musées Nationaux / Art Resource, NY.
Photo credit: Réunion des Musées Nationaux / Art Resource, NY.

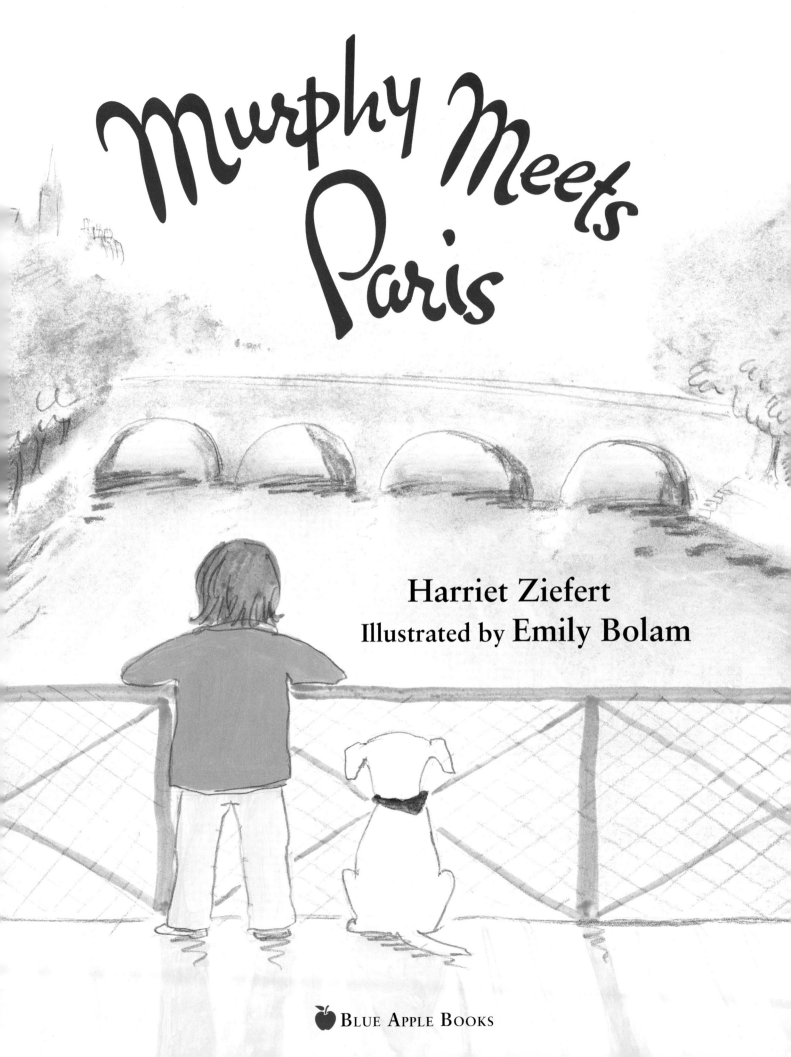

Murphy Meets Paris

Harriet Ziefert

Illustrated by Emily Bolam

BLUE APPLE BOOKS

I'm Cheryl. I am the proud owner of a yellow Labrador retriever named Murphy. Recently we went on a vacation.

By the time we got to the airport, Murphy was miserable. He traveled in a travel crate in the back of a station wagon and was not happy being confined.

I tried to explain about the trip.
"We're going to Paris."

"We have a special *Heavenly Pets* package at a four-star hotel."

"The accommodations are first class."

"You'll be taken care of by the
nice folks in baggage."

I kissed him good-bye.
"See you in Paris."

When I claimed him eight hours later,
Murphy was not speaking to me.

He was mad. I had to shove him into the taxi.

He would not say *bonjour* to the hotel doorman.

He refused to eat his dinner.

Fortunately, after a good night's sleep in a special bed, custom-covered in violet fake fur, Murphy's mood changed.

When Murphy's breakfast arrived from room service, he was all smiles.

The poached chicken with carrots, zucchini and onions, the wheat bran, and low-fat yogurt, prepared by Dominique, the hotel chef, were just what he wanted.

Murphy tried to get back into his comfy bed right after he licked his plate clean, but I said, "No, Murph. We have to get moving. There's a lot to see in Paris."

We walked from the hotel to the Luxembourg Gardens.

Murphy made himself known to several
other dogs, but they were French and wanted
no part of his American ways.

Then we went to the Louvre. There was a long queue
in front of the museum, but Murphy waited patiently.

Once inside, Murphy had no patience for sculpture
or decorative arts. He wanted to see portraits.

On the way home he insisted on posing for a street artist who had set up his easel around the corner from the museum.

Murphy stayed very still until the artist said
he was finished. Picasso could not have
had a better model!

We returned exhausted. Murphy got right into bed
and I plopped down beside him, too tired to look
at guidebooks or maps of Paris.

I ordered Murphy his second and last meal of the day, the "Dog Hamburger," ground beef with fresh carrots and green beans with a side of pasta.

It arrived with a flourish, and Murphy's manners were impeccable. He did not jump on the waiter or try to grab a taste before the gentleman was finished serving.

I decided to go out for dinner to a nearby brasserie.
I thought I'd leave Murphy in the room, but he
didn't want to be left alone, so I took him with me.

After dinner, I gave Murphy a bath. I found doggie
shampoo, along with other grooming goodies,
in a basket in the bathroom. I used them all.

I dried Murphy with the bath towel. I sprayed him with fruity perfume called *Oh My Dog*. Murphy thought he smelled delicious.

Because I wanted to sleep late, I asked
the concierge to find a baby-sitter for Murphy.

He asked the doorman, and Murphy
took the doorman for a stroll!

Afterward, the doorman took Murphy to the
agility course in the hotel's garden, but
he was not very cooperative.

I was not surprised that Murphy wasn't enthusiastic
about the exercise course in the garden.

He much prefers to use a treadmill.

We spent our third day in Paris shopping.

In Paris, dogs and their owners often
have matching accessories.

I decided to buy scarves for both of us
at *Les Cadors*, a boutique in the Marais.

How do we look?

I saved the Eiffel Tower for our last day. We took the metro, then walked to Champ-de-Mars.

Here I am trying to convince Murphy to climb the 704 steps to the second level. "It'll be worth it, Murph!"

And it was!

Then it was time to say, "*Au Revoir!*"

As we pulled away, Murphy looked back with longing.

"Do I have to do this again?" he seemed to ask.
"Unfortunately, you do," I answered.

"But I'll be waiting for you in Boston."

And I was!